THE TRIBE OF T

Koç University Press: 138 IMPRINT
ESSAY | TURKISH LITERATURE

The Tribe of the Esraris.
Ahmet Güntan

First published in Turkish in 2003 as *Esrârîler.* by Yapı Kredi Publications, and currently being published by Edebişeyler Publications, Istanbul.

First KUP printing: June 2018

Translated from the Turkish by Ali Alper Çakır
Book design: Gökçen Ergüven
Cover design: E S Kibele Yarman

Print: A4 Ofset Certificate no: 12168
Otosanayi Sitesi, Donanma Sk. No: 16 Seyrantepe/İstanbul +90 212 281 64 48

Koç University Press Certificate no: 18318
Rumelifeneri Yolu 34450 Sarıyer/İstanbul +90 212 338 1000
kup@ku.edu.tr • www.kocuniversitypress.com • www.kocuniversitesiyayinlari.com

Koç University Suna Kıraç Library Cataloging-in-Publication Data
Güntan, Ahmet, 1955-
The tribe of the Esraris (2000/2001) = Esrariler (2000/2001) / Ahmet Güntan ; translated from the Turkish by Ali Alper Çakır ; editor Emre Ayvaz.-- İstanbul : Koç Üniversitesi, 2017.
112 pages ; 13,5 x 20 cm.-- Koç Üniversitesi Yayınları.
ISBN 978-605-9389-76-1
1. Turkish poetry. 2. Turkish essays. 3. Turkish literature. I.Çakır, Ali Alper. II. Ayvaz, Emre. III. Title.
PL243.G868 E8713 2017

The Tribe of the Esraris.

(2000/2001)

AHMET GÜNTAN

Translated from the Turkish by
Ali Alper Çakır

KUP

Contents

INTRODUCTION

The Poet of Pristine Look: Ahmet Güntan

Ömer Şişman

To account for Ahmet Güntan's contribution to Turkish poetry, it is necessary to assess briefly the development of modern Turkish poetry and its main trends and tendencies. No need to say, this will not be a detailed guided tour of every single aspect of modern Turkish poetry, rather a journey through it, an overview that will have to omit some important achievements.

Modern Turkish poetry is a fascinating political phenomenon that deserves to be studied and analysed. The fact that Nâzım Hikmet, one of the leading Turkish poets, remained banned during almost 30 years, between 1938 and 1965, is in itself an exceptional event. The driving force of Nâzım Hikmet and modern Turkish poetry was politics. Hikmet wrote the first Turkish poem in free verse: "The Eyes of the Starving People" (1922). Afterwards, he *lingered* among the Russian futurists and constructivists, avant-garde cinema and theatre, he *showed interest* in folk poetry and he invented an experimental poetry. The pulses of Turkish poetry and world poetry beat together for the first time with Nâzım Hikmet.

Nâzım Hikmet's ban coincided with two important trends of Turkish poetry, Garip ("Strange", in the 1940's) and İkinci Yeni ("the Second New", from the mid 1950's to our days). In a nutshell, the poets of Garip wanted to strip poetry of its ornament and rhetoric and they turned to vernacular language, simple, understandable, and humourous. They introduced "ordinary" people, the odd folk, a childish spontaneity and things regarded as *unpleasant* in the field of poetry. It was a way to object to the thematic constraints and rigid patterns of the poetry at that time. The poets of İkinci Yeni, who grew up under the poetic influence of Garip, were influenced by the avant-garde short story-writers, especially Sait Faik. In their works, metaphors became more important. They wanted to bring back nonsense to their poems and they turned to a poetry regarded as hermetic in these years. At that time, modern Turkish poetry was exposed to francophone influences, which it transformed/interpreted; this is also probably the first time when the role of "imagery" in poetry was so often discussed.

Ahmet Güntan was born in 1955. He grew up in the 1960's, when Turkey enjoyed relative freedom characterised by many different political views and opinions. When Güntan was ten years old, the ban on Nâzım Hikmet was lifted and "Nâzım"s popularity reached its peak in the following years. This popularity and the political atmosphere of the 1960's had a strong influence on the poets of İkinci Yeni, who then dominated the poetic field.

When Güntan was young, besides Turkish literature he read many foreign authors, poets and thinkers: Duras, Beckett, Gide, Pavese, Coletti, Althusser, Kuhn, Feyerabend, Marx, Hemingway, Mann, Nietzsche, Bachelard, Whitman, Eliot, Pound, Frost, Nerval, Cendrars, Baldwin, etc. He corresponded with James Baldwin in the 1980's. In his posthumous letter signed "Your student Ahmet," he reveals how he first read Baldwin's works when he was only 14-15 years old and writes about their correspondence and the guiding influence Baldwin exerted on himself. Güntan is fully open to influences, he tries to create a family by going back and forth between Turkish and foreign authors. Yet the family that he eventually created is a kind of Addams Family for Turkey.

From the beginning, Güntan kept his distance from poetry shaped by the francophone influence. He started to read American poetry when he was 16 years old and was deeply influenced by David Bowie and Bob Dylan during his youth.

Most of the artists whom he likes and estimates are, in his own words, figures who *do not avoid contradictions*. In a country like Turkey, which has a strong tendency to polarisation, "maintaining that contradiction should not be avoided" is not easy.

From the 1980's to the 2000's, poetry in Turkey was derived from İkinci Yeni. This is what I meant when I stated above that İkinci Yeni continued almost to this day: it changed appearance but it continued. In the 1980s, images were simplified into down-to-earth metaphors, hence better understood and praised; politics was almost entirely excluded from poetry, as a reaction against the 1970s' engaged poetry. In these years, Güntan's poetry was found narrative and plain. Güntan does not fetishize metaphors. He keeps his distance from the main trends of contemporary Turkish poetry. İlhan Berk, one of the founding poets of İkinci Yeni and Güntan's elderly close friend, said: "'The stone fell down' is not a poem, yet 'The stone flew' is a poem." Ahmet Güntan thinks that this view made sense in the 1950's and that this perspective enabled the İkinci Yeni to create a meaningful language but he adds: "I was always the poet of 'The stone fell'. We had so many dreams, it's enough. The ambiguity of dreams is now circulated everywhere and so mainstream, so fundamental. Ambiguity is the fuel of the world system. The contrary, that is the straightforward look, is enlightening. If I had lived in the era of monosemy, I would have stood against it, like Valéry. But I live in a world ruled by polysemy; milliards of dollars are invested on the fortuitous polysemic spark engendered by the encounter of two contradictory words. Today we are prisoners of polysemy, we are ruled by it. The once aimed spark of the Modern–the 'beyond'–is now democratized, we all live in it, it is not illuminating anymore. Today, instead of polysemic *hermeticism*, I prefer to stand for 'thought' in poetry–not for the reward of sealed meaning but for the energetic stimulation of thinking via poetry. I am no more interested in hermetic power of clashing words which is said to be the 'essence' of modern poetry."

These thoughts drove Ahmet Güntan to write a manifesto and *Taşıyıcı Monolog.* (Pillar Monologue.) in the mid 2000s, and to author new poems, titled *Parçalı Ham.* (Fragmental Crude.). He set himself a number of interdictions:

1. Don't create the poem, look for it slowly.
2. Not inside, but outside–out in the concrete.

3. Since nobody cares about the poet, do not betray your brain chemistry for others.
4. Don't write about things that you didn't personally observe and touch.
5. Don't write about geographies that you didn't see, histories that you didn't witness [You may use the concrete knowledge coming from books as a raw material]
6. Avoid adjectives.
7. Don't make verses.
8. Don't use rhymes.
9. Beware of rhetoric.
10. Don't make implicit references. Don't rely on your reader's skills.
11. Use images in an informative way.
12. Always keep in mind the Nipper–the child yet unspoiled by the system–before writing.

In his *Pillar Monologue.*, which is almost 35 pages long, he argues that poetry has been besieged on one side by the Saucy Discourse, relying on the mediocre, and on the other side by the well-educated Intertextual Triviality; the poet has been excluded from poetry and poetry has lost its opposing force. His opinion is unequivocal: It is no more possible for the poet to stay only in the realm of poetry since it is al plundered and weakened as a literary genre. The poet is today only a faithful "Attendant" of the essential core of poetry. According to Güntan, the only space that is unconquerable is the state of poetry before it becomes a literary genre–a concrete urge in the stomach for a poetical assessment of the world. Güntan concludes that concreteness (the "touchable") is a contemporary need. Ezra Pound has a central role in the *Monologue*: "Pound's Memory with all its tensions is the starting point of a new modernity. Ezra Pound is the best craftsman ('il miglior fabbro') in modern poetry" (*Pillar Monologue.*, article 4). "The absolute freedom in the choice of subject" in the *Imagist Manifesto* is important for Güntan. He describes his concept–Pound's Memory–as a "Great intercultural storage support to the poetry that wants to find its own way" (*Pillar Monologue.*, article 99). Güntan stands against holism and reminds us that Pound's Memory is open and fragmented. He considers Mallarmé as the First Modern (*my thought has thought itself*) and Pound as the Second Modern.

He maintains that the aim of the First Modern, the *Great Insinuation*, corresponds to our present situation. According to Güntan, the First Modern's approach is "we've had enough of the power of the concrete–let's discover the subjective field of thought," whereas the Second Modern says "enough with this 'oatmeal consistency' (Pound)–let's return to the concrete–let's open poetry to dangers." Güntan sees the İkinci Yeni in Turkey as a version of the First Modern. From a superficial perspective, the time of the *Manifesto* and *Fragmental Crude.* could be considered as a rupture in Ahmet Güntan's own poetry but actually he rather lets nature take its course. Güntan was always the poet of *straight view.*

Like the main figures of his literary family, Ahmet Güntan has often been accused of being in contradiction with himself. First, he is "collectivist", "Muslim" and "gay". Then, he is opposed to identity politics and writes that he sees identity as a leash. In his own words, the bombs that the different camps throw at each other are always dropped in his lap. This is also the case of his poetry. He said that when he was young, he could write socialist poems, such as "University Cafeteria" and poems like "The best haircut I've ever had", inspired by Bowie, at the same time with the same genuineness, he adds: "This is more or less my story in poetry, I can't say that I am *in-between*, I don't like the discourse of *in-betweenness*, I don't quite understand how one can be *in-between*, I am not, I cannot be in-between. I, if I can say 'I', have connections with both of my contradictory sides, *intermittent* yet militant. To me, being in-between means being stepping back; on the contrary, I rush forward towards each contradictory side, and it is the same for poetry: on the one hand I am a formalist, for years I have been writing that form came first in poetry, that poetry needs tailoring; but at the same time, how to say, I am an *essentialist*, I never forget that my aim is to make something real, that art has a social function; I see poetry as a struggle for rights, I stand against the absolute autonomy of form in the name of which everything should be sacrificed. Actually, you know what? I think that formalism and essentialism taken separately are the refuges of the untalented. I am one of those who confront *flow* and form; flow is the *essence*, form makes one of its moments visible for everyone, it is a kind of reserving an experience aside and say 'Look here!' which is the shortest definition of poetry and literature."

Manifesto and the poems in *Fragmental Crude.* aroused various debates, Ahmet Güntan was accused of contradicting himself. This is a quite meaningful accusation for an author who wrote: "Baldwin, Dostoevsky, Pound, Nâzım, who needs a writer that does not contradict himself, who can avoid self-contradiction?" Contradiction is irreducibility. Ahmet Güntan is one of these "irreducible authors". His poetry cannot be reduced to specific themes. Let's open here a small parenthesis about the importance of full stop as a punctuation mark in Ahmet Güntan's poetry: Since his fourth book, *Romeo and Romeo.* (1995), he has added a full stop at the end of all the titles of his books and poems. In the reprints of his first three books, he didn't neglect to add these full stops. The full stop gradually lost its character of punctuation mark and was turned into a poetic sign pointing to the end of a cycle in Güntan's works. After spending his youth in a time when narrativity was despised, he transformed the titles of his poems and books into sentences in a meaningful way. Indeed, what ends with a full stop has always news value. In one of his self-interviews he mentioned that the title of the column written by Lawrence Ferlinghetti in the *San Francisco Chronicle Book Review* was "Poetry as News" and he quoted Pound's definition of literature: "Literature is news that stays news."

Besides his books of poems and his essays on poetry, in the 2000s Ahmet Güntan wrote two novels. But the most surprising work of this polyvalent author is probably *The Tribe of the Esraris..*

The Tribe of the Esraris. was first published in June 2003. It contains pieces written between July 6th, 2000 and December 30th, 2001. Each piece is dated and collected in the book in reverse chronological order. When Ahmet Güntan wrote these pieces, the Internet had just been introduced in Turkey. Güntan created a yahoogroup named "The Tribe of the Esraris" and he shared there his writings with a few Internet users.

Let's note that these pieces sometimes seem to have been written in a world without the Internet; they were written when social media did not exist, in the early days of the Internet. In these first years of the new millennium, Turkey was again in crisis: the economic crisis of 2000-2001. While the wounds of the 1999 earthquake were still fresh, major financial crises occurred in November 2000 and February 2001. In February 2001, the Turkish lira lost 40 per cent of its value. On March 3, Kemal Derviş resigned from his position at the World Bank and was appointed Minister of Economic Affairs. Until August 2002, he was responsible for negotiations with the IMF and attempted to reform the Turkish financial system. The cost of the crisis was high: the number of the unemployed exceeded two million. In addition, these years witnessed the September 11 attacks and in November 2001 the US and the UK sent troops to Afghanistan, starting a war that would last for years.

The Tribe of the Esraris. was written in those days of crisis and impoverishment. The author of the notes of *The Tribe of the Esraris.* was Esrari, an ideal figure that was praised by Ahmet Güntan. At the beginning of this book, we read the information written by Esrari, a member of the Tribe of the Esraris. Güntan declared later in an interview: "In *The Tribe of the Esraris.* I wanted to reach an ideal morality aware of the impossibility of an ideal morality, I really needed it." The grand-father of this Esrari tells us about poverty, conscience and nothingness, he comments on the expressions and images that overwhelmed us in these years, such as the "0% commission fee charged for credit cards", the "U.S. dollar–German mark crisis", the queues in front of banks and the Internet. The book is an intense questioning of poverty, a quest for conscience, not a meaningless lyric piece. In the structure of *The Tribe of the Esraris.*, in the narrative of the mystic Esrari who praises extravagantly the impossible, there is something ironical, almost grotesque. Although Güntan could easily have opted for one of the moral versions of Sufism and new age, he rejects this way and always keeps a foot in the real conditions of real life. "A romanticism that dives into a discourse about the purity of the hearts of the poor should see the poor pushing each other in a queue for free bread. How can there exist a type of material poverty that does not impoverish the heart as well?

What goodness, whose heart could withstand interminable poverty? But it is precisely the possibility of withstanding that is idealized. The possibility that goodness can persist is the conscience of humanity."

The Tribe of the Esraris. was a surprise, first unnoticed. Yet in a few years, it reached a public of readers/fans. Some books become sorts of passwords between fans. *The Tribe of the Esraris.* is now one of these. Two persons who like *The Tribe of the Esraris.* are two persons who understand each other, they belong to the same family.

Ahmet Güntan believes that the poets must be the *realists of the realists*. In an interview published in 2008, he analyzed *The Tribe of the Esraris.* in this way: "Being an Esrari is an ideal excellence, today it is impossible to be an Esrari. This is why I wrote, 'I am not Esrari but I would sign for whatever Esrari may write.' I still open it and read it, it reminds me of my values, in Istanbul being Esrari 7/24 is an impossible yet beautiful dream."

The admiration of the readers for *The Tribe of the Esraris.* became oppressive for Güntan. Finally, in *Olanlık* (Beingness), his first novel published in November 2012, Güntan creates Novice Esrari and comes to terms with being an Esrari in a discussion between Novice Esrari and Esrari:

"NOVICE ESRARI: I want to get rid of you.

ESRARI: Why?

NOVICE ESRARI: I can't stand your innocence of evil and fault, your resolution, impossible to attack you, your attachment to many inviolable things, your determination to remain kind, whatever may happen, the way you live in a totally different world. I don't know, I feel words coming from my throat, I say this man lies, if I believed you, my life would become much more difficult, but if I stand against you, would it be easier, I don't know, I am sick and tired of you.

ESRARI: Sometimes I am also tired of myself, who was the first to whisper these words in my ear? I too would like to live more casually but to my mind even casual situations are moments of decision. I keep looking for light, without being aware of it."

This kind of dialogue, which takes the readers' arguments into the fiction, is not common in Turkish literature. As an author who is estranged to his object in time, Güntan takes a coolheaded view of Esrari; he updates his work and rescues it from the deep-freezer of the past to discuss the meaning of being Esrari with his followers.

The Tribe of the Esraris. represents the questions, the answers and the quest of a poet who promised not to betray the chemistry of his brain when he was going through a deep crisis. It awaits discovery and interpretation by new readers.

Sources

Ahmet Güntan, *Esrariler.* (The Tribe of the Esraris.), YKY: 2003.

Ahmet Güntan, *Olanlık.* (Beingness.), Raskol'un Baltası: 2012.

Ahmet Güntan, *Parçalı Ham.* (Fragmental Crude.), 2nd Edition, 160. Kilometre: 2016.

Ahmet Güntan, *şiirgeldikelimedeboğuldu.* (poetryisdrownedatwords.), 160. Kilometre: 2011.

Translated from the Turkish by
Noémi Lévy-Aksu

THE TRIBE OF THE ESRARIS.

Esrari of the Esraris.

He is not a recognized person yet; he has not published a book. This is his first. Everyone who hears his name is curious as to its origins. He has nothing to do with the Alevî poet Esrârî to whom the lines "Wilst Thou Enter the Heart's Kaaba / Plunge into the Depth ye Brethren" are attributed. He came across his namesake Esrârî only after having chosen the same pen name for himself. But he liked the idea of sharing a name, so he kept it. The aspect of this pen name that arouses the most curiosity is its relation to marijuana. He claims there is no such connection, but finds it perfect that in Turkish, "esrâr" means both "mystery" and that which you use to make a joint. He took the name Esrari because he thought the world was a mysterious place. At the age of six, he found a long, thick iron rod in his backyard. He tied the two-meter-long rod at its middle to one of the boughs of an olive tree in the garden. Every so often, he would suddenly leave his playmates on the street and run to the backyard, pull the iron rod back from where it hung, then release it like a swing towards the stone wall. He would listen to the sound of it ringing until it faded away, and then do the same thing again before running back to the street to rejoin the game. "At that time I didn't even know about the word 'mystery,' but I could still understand the invitation in that sound," he says. "Short mysterious moments caught in the lulls of the game" is how he summarizes his life. He has never tried to solve this mystery; he has not gone after something he cannot solve because he has decided that this knowledge would kill the mystery. "I have a brain that feeds on ignorance," he says. More than anything else, he has arrived at where he is by watching. "I saw how, with patience, the sour grape turns into halwa," he says. Hasn't he read anything at all? No, of course he has. He cannot forget this sentence in Peyami Safa's book *Glances at the Turkish Revolution*: "The excuse that the eye cannot see itself proves false in front of a piece of looking glass." And also these words by Cemil Meriç: "From the day man put a fence around a bit of field and said, 'this is mine,' he has drifted off from the true path, murder has chased murder, catastrophe has followed catastrophe. At the end, this artificial order called civilization has been formed." One day in Behramkale, Çanakkale by the Dardanelles, under a mysterious oak tree, he finally decided to write. For the Esrari, this oak is a very important tree. Between the Kadırga Cape and the Çam Cape there is the Bük Yatağı Cape. Here, just next to the sea, there is a lonely, wise tree which casts a deep shadow. On it has been written "M7" in red paint—that is what they have written on it. "I," he says, "learned to watch the movie by myself at a very young age. When I decided to sit under that tree I felt like I was abandoning my fate, stepping into an alien land." He has found the best rendition of these feelings in Cahit Külebi. This is what the late Cahit Külebi said on television one day: "It was just as if they had laid me down and put me to sleep one night, but then I woke up." What he wrote, he wrote for a long time in this state of grogginess, he took notes in notebooks that he did not show to anyone. "I got to where I am by watching, watching and believing, watching and thinking. I also watched and wrote, with two plain eyes," he says. Those who know will understand what this means. Afterwards, he thought that from then on, he should share what he wrote, because it had become a little bit more readable. This group of people who are called the "Esraris" are more inclined towards poetry than prose, they are slow to get used to prose. To close the distance between thought and word is an old tradition of the Esraris, and it takes practice—what did they say?—everything is possible through possibility. These writings accommodate a peculiar possibility: just as their revolt seems to become explicit, they stop in their tracks and prefer to recede. Because they can recede, they allow for possibility. It might be that you reach the last page without finding anything in it. Afghanistan, for example; attention should be paid to Afghanistan. Also, the issues of honor and homeland. Those who read it closely will notice in several places a sought-after innocence. Mysterious oak, the duty is done.*

Ahmet Güntan

* In the winter of 2002, the mysterious oak burned to ashes in a fire that swept from the mountain to the sea. But it didn't die, it continues to live.

THE TRIBE OF THE ESRARIS.

Those who arrive and dwell silently, like fate.

Written by Esrari

Those who arrive like fate
silently, without intervening.
Those who show the courage of dwelling silently,
living silently and leaving silently.
Those who cannot see it fit for themselves to drivel
and drool. Those who can withstand
the terror of the eternity.
Fatalists, great fatalists,
The Esraris!

The charm mender.

Esrari, the charm mender. All things lose their enchantment one day. It is normal that this happens, but the Esrari comes and reenchants them in a way that delights the witnesses. They cannot believe their eyes; the charm has really been mended! Life with the Esrari is so delightful. If he wants to reminisce about something, he says “it was the time when olive trees were blooming.” “Just wait until the sowing season is over,” he says. The river that lies in the bosom of eternal creation flows without rushing, the person is easily enlightened about their essence, the contract of humanness is annulled. Thus is the Esrari able to mend charms, for he knows whence the charm draws its power, not from a contract but from the eternal.

December 30, 2001

Hakuna matata!* Tora Bora!

Getting cornered in Tora Bora was a part of destiny. It was going to happen either way: the sharp ledges, the endless tunnels… What jumps at you as you stare at it is a thoroughness of futility that could only have been drawn by the hand of God. Rocks, rocks, rocks, and the fury that nobody wants to understand—where else would it be crammed into other than the peak of a rocky mountain? Far away from everyone, the final days of a plain life made up of cigarettes, praying, eating, drinking, sleeping and fighting. Everyone is slightly sad because something so surprisingly plain can be loaded with this much duty.

It is said that "everything is changing too rapidly and some of us cannot keep pace." Yes, they are the Esraris, they cannot keep pace. The things that make up an Esrari are a deaf ear that comprehends neither course nor progress, and an eye that looks beyond. What do we think we will figure out, for the love of God? Are we to understand what is going on? This would be all too easy a task. We begin by looking at rocks. Then we turn to look at people, and finally at the things that happen between people. This is exactly how we know that the winds blowing on Tora Bora, like all the other winds blowing across the face of the earth, carry good news from the beloved. Do you really think that only your beloved is dear, and theirs is but a prickly pear?

December 12, 2001

---

* "No worries!" from *The Lion King*.

I did not revolt, nor did I hide.

Esrarihood is a way of becoming earthly, a way of becoming native by looking. It is the disappearance of the glue, the vanishing of the cement, the stripping off of meaning. It is a sort of being left dumbstruck. It is opposed to the trivial disrobing of the soul, to complaining, to indulging in politics. It avoids the flatterer, believing that "the flatterer cuts with a knife."* It is those who say, "let us begin by seeing it as it is," those who learn by looking, those who do not let their ideas disrupt fate, those who find the mediocre auspicious. It is those who die in the same place where they were born, those in whose name a tree is planted at birth, those who watch the world from the shadow of that tree, those who do not hesitate to talk to that tree. These Esraris are a strange bunch. They believe in the unknown but do not venture towards it, those who do not desire heaven for its blessings, those who say, "let us reunite with the place from whence we came." Esraris, the pure, the benevolent, those who reach out to the poor in their snow-covered houses not with stories of salvation but with blankets; realists who bide their time. They do not revolt, nor do they hide.

December 9, 2001

* A hadith.

Suhoor.*

Your eating schedule is changing, your sleeping schedule is changing, you are exercising a spiritual discipline that withholds you from matter, you muffle the voice of hunger by cutting your speed and slowing down, you listen slowly, you speak little; this is Ramadan, the month when the direction of the contract changes. For those who understand what we mean, the words of Nizami will make sense: "these luxuries that tickle my fancy are burdens on my back. I must kneel at the threshold of wretchedness."†

Suhoor is the preparation to retreat from today, which is administered by the secret files. Just before sunrise, it is the manifestation of the intent to not master the things illuminated by the sun, to stop, and to later close the day with plain eyes. Indeed, it is a wonderful time, just before the morning astonishment sets in. The astonishment in the face of a world illuminated by the morning light, is this not the true principle act of devotion? In a little while the day will begin, the secret files will open, the social order will resume. But those who have seized the suhoor will stand and watch as the game begins. Scurry around and see if you can find what is at the end of the road.

November 17, 2001

* Suhoor: The meal eaten before sunrise during the month of Ramadan, the next meal is eaten after sunset.

† *Mahzen-i Esrar*, Nizami.

The poet kids.

The wind blows. They make sense of the simple movements of the wind in a simple manner, they see the soul of the wind, then turn to us and one by one recount its heroic deeds. If adults listened to what was being told, they would see the metaphysics there. Some children do this, and they are the poet kids. We cannot say if they will all be poets, but the Kurds have a saying: those who see the wind also see Allah. The poet kids see the wind as well as the emptiness of this mass that Allah has gathered, and we the Esraris call such children the poet kids and we protect those we come across.

November 12, 2001

The rain.

It is the strangest form that water takes, it flows down like a string, breaks up when it hits the ground, but then the fragments separated in the sky join in a united effort to flow to their source. There is a lesson to be learned from this, of course, from this fragmented flowing. Just before hitting the soil, the drops meet with nature that surges up from the soil, they cover everything they come in contact with, wetting everything before collecting together and going back to their source. The magnificent final ceremony of water is to wet and wrap itself around all of nature.

Esrari, would you not want to pour down as rain to experience this cycle? Would you not want to be the unadulterated player of this unending cycle?

November 3, 2001

The poet's movement according to Nizami.

"Those who have knelt in the realm of the word do not prostrate themselves on every doorstep. Of their kneecaps they make feet for their hearts, and they attain union with both realms. First, their bowed heads salute their feet, and their feet and heads join to form a circle. Then, when they want to break this circle, their curved backs straighten up with a jolt of new inspiration."*

October 28, 2001

---

* *Mahzen-i Esrar*, Nizami.

Destiny.

Destiny is unavoidable. Modest or pompous, it leads you astray, it does what it wills. It is not a predetermined course—on the contrary, it spoils the predetermined course; destiny becomes perceptible through ruining and spoiling.

There was an Esrari—and as you know, Esraris believe that money should be out of the equation—wretched fellow, he had to carry a backpack full of money one day. Don't ask me why. He just had to. That day he felt the weight of money for the first time — we are literally talking about weight here, measured in kilos. And the fear that runs down his spine: what if it is snatched from him?

What will you do, my friend Esrari? It leaves as it comes. That is it, the way it is meant to be. See here, what did you observe when you went to the Fatih Sultan Foreign Money Exchange Office in Fatih with that load? The walls of the exchange office were covered with the words of Rumi, which remind the futility of this world's riches. This is destiny: did not the weight of the money you were carrying diminish for that one moment? You had gone there for a grandiose fate, but this is destiny we are talking about. It reminded you of itself, it took one step and the road changed.

October 19, 2001

The bathrobe quota.

America has lifted the bathrobe import quota it had set for Turkey, and simultaneously, there is not a single person in Turkey who is not drooling over the seven billion dollars that was given to Pakistan. Money has become a rifle held to our brow, the earth has shaken and the captain tries to save the ship. It is a tradition of the Esraris to draw a line. One should keep their fate open to the possibility of the eternal. This much curiosity about what will happen in the future is enslavement, the shackles of which are money. In a country that is enslaved by money, the bathrobe quota does not only concern bathrobe makers, but the whole population. "More bathrobes, more money," this guarantees the next maneuver of each and every one of us, whereas the Esrari knows that we are raving, approaching the barrel of the gun one step at a time with each maneuver.

October 14, 2001

The idealization of poverty.

A romanticism that dives into a discourse about the purity of heart of the poor should see the poor pushing each other in a queue for free bread. How can there exist a type of material poverty that does not impoverish the heart as well? What goodness, whose heart could withstand interminable poverty? But it is precisely the possibility of withstanding that is idealized. The possibility that goodness can persist is the conscience of humanity. "Things should not have gone this way, but unfortunately, it is the way they have turned out." Even if this phrase is the only record the conscience preserves, it is valuable. The thing that persists beyond the point of poverty, this is what the Esraris idealize. Marginal Sufism, that is to say in poverty, but a poverty that has not impoverished the heart, in a darkness that obscures all differences, I have written and I have read, and I am tired of this futile world of lies.*

October 3, 2001

* "I have written and I have read, and I am tired of this futile world of lies" is the lyrics from a folk song.

Noble Eagle, wild donkey.

Everything that happened to Benazir Bhutto... All that happened to Nawaz Sharif who succeeded her. That at the end, a general would take over. The prevention of the extension of Demirel's presidency. That there is not a voice left in either country that can question the United States of America. These things are all a part of the war; the Noble Eagle has been flying over here for many years. Tucked under its wings, secret files have been circulating from country to country. If it can still fly so gracefully today, it is because it has practically memorized the regional winds; it is easy for nobles to command the poor.

An item in the newspaper saying, "Kabul is emptying out," with a photo of villagers on donkeys. It is easier than striking two skyscrapers of course, because a man on the back of a donkey greets death more easily, just as it is easier to accept the death of a man on the back of a donkey. Difficult days await those who believe that conscience will eventually prevail, because the Noble Eagle in the sky will take a dive at the man on the back of a donkey, and the man will be hit, and the world will quickly forget.

September 17, 2001

Today Kabul is 24 degrees and sunny.

And the weather will continue like this for the next five days. This poverty stricken society has consented to a silent insulation in order to get some respite, but it appears that the silence will soon be broken again. Poor Afghans, this time fate will greet them tumbling down from the sky, despite the fact that they had accepted the cessation of all music in order to hear the pure voice from the sky. Now this silence will be broken, music will be required to suppress the crescendo of screams. The weather is nice and sunny outside. Afghanistan will be destroyed.

September 14, 2001

Orhan Kemal.

It is said that if Orhan Kemal had not been such a good-hearted man, he would have become a great author; that is to say, a good heart gets in the way of good writing. Is this not strange? In fact, a good heart is essential for good writing, for if authors cannot bring forth goodness on the day that is furthest from goodness, this means that they have lost their own battle. Succumbing to their own intelligence is something great authors cannot pull off without wounding their pride.

Orhan Kemal has a story in which a man gets on a minibus, hands the driver two and a half liras, but the driver forgets to return his change, and the man is too embarrassed to ask for it. What if he has to get off without his change? From this, a whole story unfolds as an account of poverty. Orhan Kemal is the writer of this intelligence, the author of Bekçi Murtaza. The Kurdish Arab kids from Siirt who enter Istanbul through the neighborhood of Vefa, the Akmerkez Mass Plaza shopping center in Gaziosmanpaşa, the six people who cram themselves into a car and stop on the side of the highway to drink beer, that congregation that disperses from the İsmail Ağa Mosque in Çarşamba, the kids from Gaziosmanpaşa who make a cup of tea last for hours on the top floor of the Akmerkez* shopping center... All of these people are waiting for a good-hearted author who has overcome his intelligence.

September 10, 2001

* Akmerkez was one of the first luxury malls built in Istanbul in the early 90's. Mass Plaza was a cheap alternative to the Akmerkez shopping center during the years that it was operational.

The victimhood tax.

I swear to God, money has turned into a rifle. Those who need a quick five billion* are willing to borrow it with one billion in interest due in ten days. For the person who pays this interest, this is his victimhood tax. This tax, paid by someone who is enslaved by money, is the executioner's fee. The owners of money have loaded the rifle and put the barrel of the gun to his brow, so he will either enlist in the army of the poor, or he will pay one billion in interest. So he says, "Take this tax, and in the meantime I will breathe a little and maybe find a tree-lined path that leads away from the road to poverty." He will not find it, of course.

The Esraris strongly believe that money does not just enter the pocket on its own. It comes with baggage. Money is categorically invasive, and if anything that remains when the money leaves your pocket, this is the only thing that is truly yours, and this type of impoverishment attracts the Esraris.

September 8, 2001

---

* There was a revaluation of the Turkish lira in 2005 during which 6 zeros were deleted.

1492.

America was discovered in 1492. The completion of the Sufi Lodge of Galata coincides with this. Years of pride for both cultures, the Europeans and the Ottomans... The former, for them, represents the human spirit's inclination towards progress and discovery, and the latter, for us, represents enlightenment by withdrawal and introspection so as to avoid zealotry. The same year that Europe discovers an uncharted continent and is proud of having conquered it, the Ottomans build a nest on a hill for those who take refuge in nonexistence in order to reveal the unity of existence, and they are proud of this. Today, one still invades, and the other ceaselessly, tirelessly defends its property. Among the invaders, there are some who are sick of invading and who long for silent introspection on that hill; among the defenders, there are some weary of defending and are now surrendering to the invaders.

September 8, 2001

The price of financial guarantee.

The day that the Esrari realized his financial guarantee was not valid, he rested his back against the olive. Sitting in its dark shadow, he wondered what would have happened if he had done the things necessary for his surety to be accepted. The olive, the tree that bends soundlessly under every wind that destiny brings, the tree of the Esraris, the one that does not wither no matter what, the saintly tree that has more forbearance than most since it can watch two centuries run their course. It gave tongue: "Are you grieving because you have no power? Your friend asked for a loan from someone who has money, you wanted to be his guarantor, you wanted to say that if he does not pay back you will be responsible. What did they ask you? How much you earn. They deemed your answer a complete fantasy, and said it would not do. Are you grieving for this?" "Should I rejoice then?" asked the Esrari. "Yes," said the olive. "Rejoice, because you changed the course of your effort years ago. When everyone put up booths at the market you took yours away, when everyone shouted you kept silent, and when everyone turned on the lights you turned them off, you slept at sunset and awoke at sunrise, you carried your home to the place between two horizons. The path changed, you changed. Why should they accept your financial guarantee now?" Look at the olive and follow its example. If water was present it grew, and if not it withered, bending in the wind. Eventually it sprang back to life and now it waits for the day of judgment—did you not choose its deep shade for this reason? "Yes," said the Esrari, for he had understood. "I am no longer using my effort to suppress anyone's cry, this is why I am an Esrari in a cool, silent shade."

August 31, 2001

In the shadow of sultans.

In Tünel, on Galipdede Street, the mausoleum of Sheikh Galib. Next to him is İbrahim Müteferrika. In Fatih, the teahouse covered with grapevines* on Yedi Emirler Street. In Beşiktaş, between the pier and the municipal repository, the high-reaching old poplar. In Süleymaniye, the Cherry Tree Mosque Street.

In Gaziosmanpaşa, the Mass Plaza. The tomb of Abdülmecid the Second. In Sultanahmet, next to the cistern, the stone that marks the center of the world. In Bebek, the front of the Turkish Bank of Commerce, in the Bebek Mosque's yard, the shorn cypress that competes with the minaret. In Fatih, the Flash Internet Cafe. Poet-spirited, sweet tempered Sultan Ahmet. Ziya Gökalp. Necip Fazıl. Sait Faik. The Africans. The Bangladeshis. The Kurds. The Zazas. The Arabs. The militant victims.

August 24, 2001

* The grapevine was later chopped down during road maintenance. It was a beautiful old grapevine.

The traffic accident.

Two lovers are inside a car when it suddenly starts swerving. One is at the steering wheel, the other in the passenger seat. The driver is locked onto the road, but if he could find the time he would embrace his lover next to him. The careening seems to last forever, first they hit another car, then a wall, then yet another car, everything that was going slowly until that instant suddenly becomes rapid — bam! bam! then another bam!, then everything abruptly stops. "When the runaway train comes to a halt, that is the human condition,"* a magical instant when the surrounding rumble is inaudible, then the world slowly regains its original rawness. Consciousness softens again, the hustle and bustle, the mundane things return. Except for one thing, the thing that does not return to being raw, that is, when the car was swerving from side to side, the hand that the lover put on the driver's neck to protect it from the impact. That hand, the only thing left from the metaphysical retreat, that hand… It reminds us that on the path to disappearance the strongest unity is love.

August 20, 2001

---

* *İki Şahit ve Diğerleri* (Two Witnesses and the Others) by Haldun Bayrı.

The pure language of conscience.

The Esraris struggle to be as pure as poetry, because for the Esraris, poetry is the sole instance of justice and equality.

The Esraris' quest brings to mind another quest of humanity: politics. But politics idealizes justice, and thus, it is completely outside the realm of poetry. First of all, it is not pure like poetry, because it belongs to a stranger. Somebody has stepped forward and said, "My people, let us unite in justice and progress towards equality." This has nothing to do with poetry.

The concept of the people is a construction, it was needed and thus it was contrived. He who has demonstrated his ability to construct has the right to rule the construction. Politics is the need to reign, that is all. However distant we were to justice and equality before becoming a people, we are just as distant now.

For an Esrari, it is his own conscience, the pure language of this conscience, that brings him closer to justice and equality. Politics is a hollow fancy, a filthy drivel.

August 13, 2001

Poetry in Esrarihood.

Some live, write, live, write, live, write. And some live, refrain from writing, live, refrain from writing, live, refrain from writing, and then write. Those who live and write are authors, those who live and resolve not to write are poets. Poetry is written by forgetting, and if this were not so there would not be such a thing as Esrarihood. The Esraris started out on a quest for knowledge but arrived at a poetry nourished by ignorance.

August 13, 2001

The Cherry Tree Mosque Street in Vefa.

There are some who view politics as the implementation of humanistic ideals on a day-to-day basis. For them, politics is a struggle for a beautiful world befitting humanity. "After the invention of the truck, nothing will be the same!", "Human dignity will overcome torture!", "A bright future awaits Turkey if it embraces the age of knowledge and rationalism!" We know the ideals, so be it, what is there to say? We have no objections.

In Vefa, under the great shadow of the Süleymaniye Mosque, lies the street of the Bangladeshis, the street of the bedsitters where the Bangladeshis stay, having tumbled over from their country. Perhaps we should ask them about the human dignity that is supposed to overcome torture. Perhaps they would explain better the art of staying on one's feet, that history is shaped through this art, and that in politics the winners are the ones who spit the most. Then they would go to sleep in their communal rooms with full bellies, unaware of the privileged youth's dreams of a better world. The funny thing is that if they were the powerful, they would be doing politics, they would be spitting into the pot, and when their desire to dominate reared its head, they would need an ideology. There cannot be politics without spit, and those who say otherwise are the ones who believe in their very own progressivist chronology. The Esraris do not believe in a history of this sort. They believe in blind history. For those who want to see the unchanging fortune of humankind, the way passes through the Cherry Tree Mosque Street in Vefa, under the shadow of Süleymaniye.

August 12, 2001

To pass the day.

You wake up in the morning. You are either one of those who wish to wake up to something big, who desire a day that reminds them of their purpose in this world, a day that will take yet another step towards the ultimate goal of life. Or, you desire a day that is uncluttered by the vanities that serve as the paste, you survey what is beyond before looking at what is at hand. You desire a day that has resolved to bury into the night everything that it will collect, that is ready to gamble for the eternity. If the latter holds, you are one of the Esraris. They seek the nondescript, the mediocre. An agenda is the unripe dream of those who imagine they have the ability to influence the course of events. The true sovereign knows he cannot master fate, and does not need to pass the day in pursuit of a goal. Only when a match can light without being struck does its fate change, and it can become something other than a match.

August 7, 2001

The Black Sea fig and the Aegean fig.

Esraris have always held the fig tree in great esteem. At some point, it was observed that the further north one goes, there emerges a difference between the fig that grows in the Black Sea's green, all-enshrouding light and the fig that grows in the Aegean's humble, white, all-illuminating light. The Black Sea fig is darker and more aggressive. If you tear its branch off, the bark quickly twists back, covering the wound; it is a warrior. The Aegean fig is wise; it is a pacifist, it does not know how to bandage its wounds. It grows just like that, heedlessly, flexing and arching. Thus it ages, emanating a sense of peace all the while. The Black Sea fig, like all northern trees, believes in the power of exploration. It spreads its branches left and right to explore. The Aegean fig stays where it is, becomes earthly, becomes a native through observation, sheds all significance and waits to be discovered. It does not waste a single negative remark on the course of things. The principal tree of the Esraris is the Aegean fig. World history is not the history of explorers as we have been taught, but as the Esraris believe, it is the history of those who wait to be discovered.

August 6, 2001

The culture precipice.

Two humans sculpted from the same clay, but raised in different cultures: the same words mean different things to them, and they both say, "my way or the highway." This is absurd but we encounter it all the time; there are even those among us who claim superiority because of this—they are dreaming.

Two steep precipices facing one another. In the middle there is a rift that complicates crossing. Both sides have to shout to communicate. The voices echo, words fly back and forth, two distinct cultures on either side and no possible truce.

The Esraris have been saying this since the beginning: make some water run into this rift. If you can make some water run into it, the danger will subside. A unity against the void, a love for Being, these are what the water brings.

Once upon a time the Esraris assembled, young Esraris, like unripe figs on the branch, angry at the curses coming from the other side of the rift. Noticing that a fight was about to break out, an Esrari elder shouted: "Is it not us who have survived so many precipices without a scratch and lived so long, is it not us who have acted as fathers to the murderers of our grandfathers, become partners with our robbers? Stop, sit down, you are kin to the Esraris. We are completely immune, the snake does not bite us, and scorpions' poison does not affect us. Remember your uncle who shut the door so that you would not scream at the sight of the snake? What did you see when the door opened, had your uncle not grabbed the snake and brought it to us?"

So this is how we Esraris are, a veritable confection of good will. Good to some, bad to others, but free from precipices.

July 25, 2001

Conscientious lads, conscientious lasses.

What they say might tickle your fancy—after all, they are opposing the global dominion of money by putting their lives on the line. Then, they are all beautiful youths, obviously they all study at good schools. Conscientious lads, conscientious lasses in lovely clothes. Wherever rich countries meet, there they go to oppose the management of poor countries under the aegis of globalism.

If you live in a country that is well acquainted with the IMF and the World Bank, you have the right to ask: what changed so suddenly? Seriously, what happened? Why are these youths now opposing the global establishments led by their own countries? Let us say that they just woke up, and their conscience opposes their countries' impoverishment of others. But if they are so sensitive to poverty, why can they not see the poverty in their own countries, like America? The Mexicans in Los Angeles, the blacks in Texas, the Native Americans in the Dakotas? We can see them all the way from here. The exotic poor are probably more acceptable.

The Esrari is confused, the poor understand one another, but then a trend comes along and everyone jumps on the bandwagon!

July 22, 2001

Özal.*

The most dazzling front page the secret files have ever chosen. Big hopes. It is such a fertile front page that everybody sees themselves in him, the famous question of the "four tendencies": we have united, we were victorious over archaism, we are progressing, and we are catching up with the rest of the humanity. It is such a compelling button to press. It offers human rights to the educated, money to the uneducated, and Lucky Luke to the jaded intellectuals. It collects us, lifts us up, and makes us flow into the channel that the secret files want. A terribly fertile button on a sensitive point of society's nervous system. It is not like the buttons they make nowadays, when you press this one you do not have to press anything else. It is he who led the communists into the abstract labyrinth of human rights, the Islamists into the labyrinth of Americanism, the nationalists into the labyrinth of not seeing the state as sacred. Lots of loans were taken to achieve this. Today we see that the secret files did not give these loans to him in vain. He was a very good investment, a very practical mind. He was never a fatalist, we should have guessed from that alone, he would never be at a loss, he would always readily conjure up a solution. Thus he is a far cry from the Esraris.

July 21, 2001

* Turgut Özal was the 26th Prime Minister of Turkey from 1983 to 1989. He established the Motherland Party with the premise of uniting these four tendencies: the democratic left, the liberal right, the nationalist right and the Islamic right.

Ninety percent humidity, 40 degrees centigrade.

When the temperature reaches forty and the humidity ninety percent, the true course of mankind's adventure on the face of the planet becomes clearer. When nature shows its unforgiving face, neither politics nor money will remain! Everything has stopped to wait for this murderous weather to pass. The only ones who can detach themselves from the lethargy of life taken hostage by the heat are those who can spend their day in a room with air conditioning. In those chilled rooms, now separated from the deer trail of humanity, are unimpeded discussions about money, the IMF, Kemal Derviş,* abstract things like the technocratic government. But for those without air conditioning, who have to spend the day face to face with the heat, life will show its truest aspect: when the air conditioning breaks down, we are all equal.

Heat, counter to expectations, brings about the concrete, and air conditioning, the abstract.

July 17, 2001

---

* Kemal Derviş is a Turkish economist and politician. After a 22-year career at the World Bank, he was invited to Turkey to become the Minister of Economic Affairs in March 2001. During that time, Turkey was facing its worst economic crisis in modern history.

The pious nihilist.

One is Cioran, the nihilistic one, who thinks that the ideal is an "effacement," that is to say, a well-calculated self-effacement, and this, he says, no one can accomplish anyway. The other one, the pious one, Dostoevsky, says there is a single thing that can withstand cynicism forever, and that is the religious "existence of something else." For Dostoevsky mercy is perhaps the only law of human life, whereas for Cioran what is mercy but one of the failings of goodness?

Let's imagine they came next to one another, in the same body, both the nihilist and the pious. They both see the futility, and do not find a loneliness in this futility. This would be a good description of Esrarihood: do not raise your hopes, do not fall for the social contract, love those who are victimized by the contract.

July 6, 2001

Morning Esraris.

That grandson of the old Esraris, who pensively smokes his morning hookah with his morning coffee while looking at the morning sun reflecting off the morning pool. He would lose nothing of his poise if the world suddenly collapsed. He has woken up early, experienced the unpopulated astonishment that early birds experience, prepared himself for the day using this astonishment, and is now waiting for the people. Like a tree, he is digging into the place where he stands. Go around the world and come back, he is still there, waiting for the world to come to him from across an even wider gap. In a world where the SUV and the sushi people roam at night and wake up late in the morning, he has found the shade of a tree early in the morning, a hookah, a cup of coffee, a bit of water to watch, and a dream that awaits him at home. A perfect constancy, what more could you want? Someone with bad eyes once said: the malice of day is better than the benevolence of the night. This is what the morning Esraris know.

May 30, 2001

The lap of the dynamic troupe.

I am an Esrari. I cannot remember when it happened, but I suddenly found myself lodged in this tradition.

I watched for a very long time, "for a long time I used to go to bed early,"* I thought for a very long time, my life was spent like a holiday in the arms of ignorance, I raised my head and looked from above, I surmounted a wall made from my own clay, found myself inside a tradition, I let go, and all is well. I will keep looking for a long time, I will climb over the wall of flesh and leave, I will say to those who are speeding "stop a little, slow down," we will let go, we will amble about, because those who progress eventually sit onto the lap of the dynamic troupe.

May 22, 2001

---

* Proust.

A Taliban unaware of anything.

The soldier of a belief, tied to one place—dust and dirt—cannot see what is ahead. The past is full of turmoil. What did you do for Afghanistan today? I defended it. I forbade the keeping of birds, the flying of kites on rooftops. And no music either. We need to rest for a while, we were flung from place to place, and we are weary. I went against destiny, fought to stop time. Esraris, you asked these questions on my behalf, there must have been some snappy responses. But you should know this: I am unaware of anything. I have chosen to sleep together with my people. I have brought the silence of the mountains down to the city. If there are those who control what will happen when I wake up, know that they are the enemies of sleep. Those who do not know the joy of waking up do not know the eagerness of those who lay down to sleep. I am unaware of anything. Esraris, I am a Taliban unaware of anything.

April 29, 2001

Listen: what does the voice of your conscience say?

For a long time the domination of money has known no competition, it is money that we are fixated on, those SUVs and SUV drivers that pass by with unshakable gravity. The dynamic troupe that makes up the "Akmerkez Protection Society" is making money. If we are to look where money is being spent, we see that money does not enter the pocket on its own, but enters together with other things. The philosophy of the Esrari fathers that said "Don't let money ride on your back, but ride on its back yourself" has all but disappeared. Before, people at least had the chance to taste equality at school, and this weakened the domination of money. Now rich children and poor children are separated as babies. The doctors are separate, the schools are separate, the neighborhoods are separate, and now even compulsory military service has been segregated. How long has this domination lasted? Alright, we invented money and got excited, we said "let them do, let them pass." Was it too much to hope that we have had enough humanity to tire of talking money day and night? Can we not think for a moment where we would be without progress?

March 28, 2001

Those who eat the cream of hardship.

He who has woken up to face a void with hardship and then been able to stave off the hardship by diving into an issue he believes in, who has been able to spread on top of a bare slice of bread butter that first and foremost tastes good to him, who has been able to eat his fill with good appetite, may he know that he is a beloved servant of God. But what about those who keep staring at that empty slice of bread? Those who, through this staring, sever themselves from time and space and, in their hopelessness, beg to God? Those who exhaust themselves by watching and understanding? Those who cannot overcome the tedium. Why were we deemed deserving of this futility? How far the cream of hardship is from us. Other than God, what can we believe in? So be it: let us keep tally by believing, putting out feet up and eating the cream of hardship.

March 26, 2001

The secret files.

What we hear and see all day is not secret. The things that are very secret but could come to light at any moment, or the things that may one day eventually come to light, are not secret either. Those who rule the world, and how they rule it are secret. So the secret files belong to them, and unless some madman shows up, we will never learn about them. So how do we know about the existence of these files that we will never encounter? Because those in charge always press the same buttons, and sometimes they press so many rational buttons in a row that it becomes clear somebody is pressing them. Moreover, societies that have experienced long periods of turmoil sense the existence of the secret files. For example Afghanistan, a country at war for 30 or so years, has finally tired of being dragged around by the secret files, and it has closed its gates, consenting to the Taliban. Afghanistan has chosen to remain as a country where everything is forbidden. Poor Afghan society, after a short respite it too will miss McDonald's. In the secret files, every possibility has its weapon. McDonald's entered Turkey in 1987 through Taksim. The secret files got their foot in the door. Today's children, growing up in Yahya Kemal's neighborhoods without calls-to-prayer, who have no idea about Ahmet Haşim's "Muslim time", are America's most powerful weapon. Perhaps we will see where it leads, but since the real secret files will never come to light, what we will see will not be a secret file. The council that manages the very "raw age"* is definitely smarter than us.

March 16, 2001

---

* Behçet Necatigil, a leading Turkish poet known for his laconic style as well as his later experimental works.

The US dollar–German mark crisis.

You will not encounter a crisis among the Esraris. Esrarihood is the appropriation of the factors that can lead to a crisis. They are stolen away and thrown somewhere nobody will be able to use them, trivialized until they become irrelevant. Maybe somebody should admit that within the paradigm that the dollar-mark consciousness has placed us in, one needs a few dollars and marks to protect oneself from the dollar-mark consciousness. What if one has no dollars and no marks? When dollars and marks shake the dust off their feet and create a crisis, what should be done then? Alright Esraris, show us your sense of belonging. Find yourselves the best companions against the crisis. The companions are the poor. It may be raining here, but it is hailing in Zeytinburnu. So the Esrari will idealize his companion, poverty. Everybody who is opposed to the dollar-mark consciousness needs to idealize poverty.

January 26, 2001

The front of the Turkish Bank of Commerce in Bebek.

There are holes in the city, passageways that suddenly transport you to a completely different neighborhood. The front of the Turkish Bank of Commerce in Bebek is one of these. Passing by, you will suddenly cross into the street in Vefa lined with bedsitters. There are always five or six youths waiting there. Their fathers have felt the disillusionment of their grandfathers, and they in turn feel the disappointment of their fathers, and now they are waiting for a job in Bebek.* The inhabitants of Bebek do not look at them. If somebody makes eye contact, the youths will stare them down with sexually charged defiance. For the majority of people walking by, they are six pairs of old shoes. Nobody remembers that there are human feet inside those shoes. Those torn shoes open the Bebek-Vefa channel. The passerby will avert his gaze, look own and watch those shoes, then rapidly lift his head back up and close the channel. What's done is done.

February 20, 2001

* Bebek—perhaps the richest neighborhood in İstanbul—and Vefa—a humble historic district by the Golden Horn—are located in different parts of the city.

The need to return to God.

Esrari, why did you turn your back on so many things that you value? In order to rejoin my essence. Was everything that I value not turned into a cause by the powerful? For example, I always read, do I not? That means the right to be informed is dear to me, but do you not see what later happened? The right to be informed was turned into a cause, others took ahold of it, and those others are not dear to me. So, when I turn my back to an equality that they described as "equality can sometimes be unjust,"* does it mean that I have given up on equality? No, just the opposite, I returned to my essence. When a stranger took ahold of that which was mine, I did not fight him, since that would have meant doing unto the stranger what he did to me. Pose the question like this: Esrari, why did you become an Esrari? So that I would not venture so far from the shore as to not be able to return.

February 9, 2001

---

* Rahşan Ecevit. She is the wife of Bülent Ecevit, a Turkish social democrat ex-prime minister.

Farewell, my beautiful friend.

They asked an Esrari if he could list in order the deaths of the 10 people he loved the most? He ordered them indeed, by descending age, but then a pain of separation stabbed his heart, because he saw that at the top of the list were his mother and father, for they are the eldest after all. How futile, he thought, you come and then you go. It is said that everyone leaves something behind. So who orders the things left behind by the dead? Curious, because soon the turn comes to those who had ordered what was left behind. Memories empty one by one as we go down the list, everything sinks into the void. As we discuss if it was like this or like that, the painful news has already arrived. Dead, but someone from the bottom of the list. The Esrari understood that there is no order to this business. When your turn comes you take off, but turns are not based on age. Then it would be smart not to believe what we are told about what happened and how it happened in the past, thought the Esrari, if not even death follows a list. Listen to me, you who point at the distance as if there is a road leading to social paradise! Are you confident in the list and the path? You jumbled the order, taught us something important, you were the first to rescue himself from the lap of futility. Farewell, my beautiful friend.

January 29, 2001

The pain of separation.

They are so close to you that you have become accustomed to living without looking at them. You are so sure that you are made from the same substance—what could you gain by looking at them to remind yourself of this? Esraris, do you know a tale of separation? We wish that there was no such thing as separation. Those made of the same substance should not be separated. If there exists a path, those behind should not be separated from those ahead of them. The pain of separation, the only true pain. The altering and ending of interactions. Being forced to accept life. The prayer for this futility to not be meaningless. If you are an Esrari and the process of separation has begun, what can you do? Are you going to drown the pain of separation? No, Esrari, you will not bury it; you will hold it by the hand and suffer it, because the pain of separation is the only true pain.

January 4, 2001

For whom will we grieve?

Politics idealizes justice. The Esraris, who long ago turned their backs to any ideology, had also turned their backs to politics and to a justice that consequently becomes an ideology. They had said that the only true justice is that of the conscience. There will always be those who spin tales high and low, the Esraris do not acknowledge them. Today, seeing what happens in the prisons that the state has broken into by following its own ideology of justice, the Esraris understand well that the only real refuge for justice is their own conscience. With all that is happening, for whom will we grieve? For those dying for their ideals, being burnt, setting themselves on fire? For those dying for their ideals without being able to make them heard? For those naive enough to mistake history for a chain of struggles to reach an ideal heaven worth dying for? Should we grieve for these beautifully pure souls who are pawns in the giant power struggles whose players are far from pure? For the hearts that are also destitute from prolonged poverty? For those who refuse to soften even in the face of these poor hearts? For those who scream slogans about that distant heaven as they die for it? That these slogans vanish without being heard? For which one of these should we grieve?

December 22, 2000

Facing up to oblivion.

However much you were able to see and hear, however much you managed to think, managed to gather and declare "these are the things I will leave behind," however much you were able to view as a source of hope, that you incorporated and were able to claim "these are the things that constitute me, that separate me from the others," however proficient your speech was, however many blessings you received, however much you salvaged and took pride in, however much you reached out, however pleasing the sound that you produced was, however much you could proudly give up, however much screaming you could withhold, however much justice you deserved, can you surrender all this? Can you face up to being forgotten and go beneath the soil like a perfect sacrificial victim? Can you stand one step behind that ineffable truth and be the perfect subject who accepts a casual farewell?

November 12, 2000

The wire transfer counter.

"Dear Brother,

I have not seen you since I started my work at the bank. And it looks like it will be difficult for us to see one another from now on because we start at nine thirty and finish at six in the evening. The bank does not have any paper suited for writing a proper letter either. This is why I am writing on this piece of scrap paper.

They put me at the 'acrèditifs' counter. Actually, it is a simple job, but not a duty to give to a person with white hair who said on the day that he started, that he has had no dealings with finance whatsoever. I get bored, I feel ashamed and I feel like a man standing there stark naked. A Jewish or a Greek child could do this job easily, whereas I tremble here, afraid of making a mistake. Then you have to converse with the customers. Some are impolite, some vulgar, some irascible, some haughty; with all of them you must be polite, lenient, smiling and reverent like a 'barber' or an innkeeper's apprentice.

In spite of everything, I think I can tolerate this situation for a week at most. I will explode. I am writing these lines both to share my troubles and to ask for advice as I anticipate the hour when I will take my topcoat and leave the bank, never to return. Would you not come to visit me for a minute if you find the time? You can ask for the "Wire Transfer Counter" at the door."*

November 20, 2000

---

* A letter from the poet Ahmet Haşim to the novelist Abdülhak Şinasi Hisar.

The Tüyap book fair.*

An amusement park for books. You would have to be a child to go and enjoy it. Those merry-go-rounds! Those haunted houses! Those bumper cars! That hall of mirrors! That Spanish woman's skirt! Does an Esrari come across new books at fairs? Ask them, and let them answer: do you Esraris encounter new books at fairs? "No, we first encounter a new book in our heads, and then we search and find it. For us, the latest book is the last book that our search has led us to. We are the Esraris because we listen to these voices."

November 13, 2000

* TÜYAP is the name of a large convention center in Beylikdüzü, İstanbul.

The void and poverty in Mustafa Irgat.

From the flesh, a spark in the void, the mirror touched the nose
The fingers gave a blank salute, the stain of the moonlight shimmered in the rain;
The game of carrying your poor waist is the light raining in its light.

November 7, 2000

You too believe, and you too will possess God.

God is the absolute possessor, the absolute verdict holder. It is only in people's hearts that He is the absolute supreme. For those who ask, "does He exist?", the answer is already "no, He does not." The absolute supreme is only reached by believing. Because of this, for those who believe, God is beyond dispute, and they do not have to prove his existence to anyone.

November 7, 2000

What would you do if you had three months to live?

They once asked an Esrari elder: What would you do if you had three months to live? “I would just stand there and look,” replied the Esrari, “like I always do. I would watch and wait for my time to come to an end. Also, I would pray that death brings the absolute.”

This is the conscience of an Esrari elder who is free of all burdens—a clean conscience.

November 7, 2000

The lucky cream of the crop.

The Esraris are strange people; one of their habits resembles that of autistics. You have to teach them everything; they cannot figure things out on their own. Let us put it another way: if you leave them alone they will come up with something completely unexpected, because coming up with nothing wouldn't do either, the mind would tear apart from fear. If you do not leave it to them but teach, they will learn well and figure out the mathematics of it. They can apply this math better than anyone else, for they are the cartographers of humanity, and their map is a detailed one indeed. The lucky cream of the crop likes this about them, they like the Esraris' enthusiasm for learning. But the Esrari style of interpretation that happens when they are left alone, now this will not do, because this is the way of the heart, beloved to the Esraris. The lucky cream of the crop does not like this, for when consciences speak the cream does not foam.

November 6, 2000

Hey, people!

Can an Esrari reach the point where, in order to suppress his inner doubt, he raises his voice to shout “Hey, people!” to guide his neighbors? This would be ridiculous, why would an Esrari suppress his inner doubt? Why should he waste time suppressing the doubt when can simply skip over it? The Esrari is a believer, by skipping over doubt he will reach benevolence. But you Esraris are too nice. Perhaps we are, but this is what we want, that nobody would go around shouting “Hey, people!”

November 3, 2000

Sickness according to Cemil Meriç.*

"As you know, I do not believe in sickness. Sickness is a revolt of the organism, a revolt against life. When the chasm separating the real and the ideal widens, either biology forces the mind to listen, the organism continues its dark and feral life, the mind turns off its lamps and sanity goes out the window. Or, the mind turns on all its lamps, the body revolts and goes on strike against itself, commits harakiri. Sickness does not visit the neighborhood of those who truly love, who are truly loved, who do not have frightening and unsolvable contradictions between their dreams and their lived lives. Sickness: the snapping of strung wires; sickness: the taking of refuge at a harbor; sickness... What do we care about sickness."†

October 29, 2000

* Cemil Meriç (1916-1987) is a Turkish conservative author and translator.

† *Jurnal*, Vol. 2.

I could crumble these mountains with a sigh.

Those stone mountains that stand without budging… If I were to sigh they would definitely understand me. Who knows, maybe they feel sorry for me? "Look at that Esrari, he can look in the mirror and see how fate is aging him, but he cannot understand our fate, how we age, because we age much more slowly than he can perceive." Is the outcry of the Esraris a weak one? Whatever they do, they are unable to pass into the domain of eternity, but they believe and they wait. A duty has been accepted, which will continue to burden them. So many sighs have accumulated in the Esrari that if he sighed but once, those mountains would crumble. How else would change ever happen?

October 24, 2000

Fear.

When someone experiences fear, does he feel it at that instant when he thinks he has broken his ties with everything? Oh Esraris, are you never frightened? Yes, we are, for we know well that instant when you break your ties with everything. It is a dark moment. It is not different for believers either. They also fear. It is a grave pact you make when you agree to be human. When the pact is broken, one becomes frightened—it really is scary! Let go of your fear Esrari, you are familiar with it already. Is this not why you have become an Esrari? At one point you thought you broke your ties with everything, and then disappeared.

October 17, 2000

There is a bankruptcy in every Esrari's childhood.

A foreclosure official—a person whom the government has employed because of the debt your father could not pay—will come to the house where you live in order to confiscate your belongings. The furniture is smuggled to the upstairs neighbor. You can never forget the mark left behind by the wall clock. So it happens like this: when this thing called money is lacking, somebody knocks on the door, takes your belongings. Then there is somebody else called the fiduciary whose task is to retain the things taken from homes. Everything can change all at once, mothers and fathers can suddenly be left powerless, the father can be left unemployed, the neighbors above can help stash belongings away from the foreclosure official.

Years pass. The child who discovered the insecurities of life very early on will only be able to find security again in his conscience. The river will run and the waters will change, but something that endures must also exist. Divine justice, the mystery of existence, absolute beauty, the equality that fate brings. For those who are aware, all these concepts exist within the conscience. For the Esraris, the only nest that existence has made for itself is the conscience, for as children they have seen the wound opened by a lack of conscience.

October 16, 2000

Fresh beginnings.

Sometimes it happens. You want to move aside, somebody thinks it is a game. First their voice is heard, the serenity is broken, then they arrive in person, the wire snaps, the harmony is corrupted. As you keep saying no, the invitations multiply and the issue becomes convoluted. You remember why you escaped, why you wanted to move aside in the first place. For the Esraris, there are no surprises in this world. For this reason they have become friends with that eerie monotony, and all invitations are in vain. In the face of that enormous void, there are those with whom they care to partner up and those with whom they do not. They avoid partnerships and the tiresome contract. What does the Esrari care what anyone says? When one listens to oneself, one does not hear the sound of a contract. If there is a mirror that deserves to be looked at, it is the mirror that Shams of Tabriz held up to Rumi. This is the mirror that allows a brief fresh beginning amidst all the monotony.

We do not domesticate our revolts, but our style is to always listen with one ear to the silence. We Esraris see no great art in complaining.

October 10, 2000

Quitting evil cold turkey.

I beheld the cannibalism of the average mind; so today I quit evil cold turkey. There is nothing good about our ideas obstructing fate. If you keep your ideas to yourself, you will not salivate like a cannibal. The good is absolute and it is ultimately rewarded. Tolerating evil brings you nothing. When was it decided that cruelty brings you anything? The only thing that tolerating evil brings about is drooling. The saliva of the average mind is potent. Those who do not want to see spit, cease tolerating the foul. The Esraris like to set out on the path but leave where the path ends to fate.

October 5, 2000

Müslüm Baba.*

He is an accordionist, but he has lost his instrument. If only he could find his accordion, his bodily movements would no longer be awkward since he would be playing the accordion. He uses his voice instead of the accordion now. This soft voice can only exist when he performs these bizarre movements, because only then does Müslüm Baba's invisible accordion play. And a strange resignation that comes with it: I'll play my accordion and leave, for I am a fatalist.

October 3, 2000

---

* Müslüm Gürses is a popular singer.

A mirage in the desert.

These words belong to Devlet Bahçeli:* "An ideal idealist is like a mirage in the desert."

And these ones are the utterances of the *Yeni Binyıl*† journalist Ferhat Kentel about the anti-globalization protests in Prague: "Some things are changing. And in a very radical way indeed. Yesterday in Seattle, today in Prague, finally some people have begun to poke their fingers into the eye of the problem. These people are lifting the ostentatious mantle that overlies globalization. Finally there is a real language to stand up against the dominant neoliberal ideology. This language is subverting the ethics forced on us by capitalism."

Isn't it great? They are both searching for an ideology.

Let us listen to Cioran answering them: "Inside every person slumbers a prophet, and when he wakes up, the evil in this world multiplies a little more."

October 1, 2000

* Devlet Bahçeli is an ultra-nationalist politician, who has been the chairman of the Nationalist Movement Party (MHP) since 1997.

† *Yeni Binyıl* is a newspaper. The events alluded to are the anti-capitalist protests in Prague during the IMF and World Bank summits in September 2000.

The flame shivering in the lamp has the chills.*

The lamp shifts its gaze from the people taking shelter in its light towards the deep darkness that begins after the furthest point it is able to illuminate. How important it is for people, and how they struggle for the burden of leadership in the light of its flame—a flame that cannot even warm itself! It shivers, it shudders, it knows that it is nothing at all, the cold flame flickering in the lamp.

September 28, 2000

* From the folk song "Mihriban" by Abdürrahim Karakoç.

Humanity whose three fingers point at itself.

It is God who brings about all that is. Because God brings about all that is, the things he brings about—all things that exists—are in unity. In the unity of nature there is no fear of God. But humanity, which has reached down to the bottom of bedrock, has separated from the unity of those rocks to such an extent that it asks this ignorant question: "If these rocks cover the earth, why then have they stopped and gone mute?" Because they are leaning. For humans have also covered the earth, but they do not stop, lean and cease talking. Instead, they always crave a greater authority. Even if they managed to become united, the only thing worth fearing would still be God.

I am afraid my child, that it is true what you said about humanity pointing at itself with three fingers while it points with the index finger at anything else. And, if it uncurled those three fingers towards the thing at which it points, it would not be pointing anymore but extending its hand.

I have heard about a practice called *inşirâh-ı sadr*: the posthumous removal of the heart from the chest cavity for the purpose of purification.

September 20, 2000

Tomato, pepper and eggplant.

The observations of the wandering Esrari.

A very unhappy young man with his head stuck between two speakers, is singing along with the Müslüm Gürses song he is listening to. The high-spirited airport maintenance crew that is having dinner like a family in the humble dining room built right next to the garage toilets as if there were no other place left in the giant airport. The shortbread cookies that have died with their maker. The Internet café where they take shoes off at the door. The dark majestic plateau that says "come, join me." The bitter energy that the eternal imposes on people. The divine balance that is tipped from left field by the ringing of a cell phone. The innocent way a boy looks at his uncle. The fig tree that now belongs to someone else. The fleeing snake that cannot see that the human is also fleeing it. The fleeing human that sees the snake is also fleeing him. Tomato, pepper and eggplant.

September 20, 2000

The voiding of the bowels.

Having full bowels is a moment of equality. You are equal to everyone, since all bowels fill, of course. Every once in a while your bowels empty so well that you end up feeling light as a feather. Now, this does not happen to everybody all the time, so it cannot be considered equality. At such moments, a beautiful possibility appears before you and a certain inertia takes you over. Maybe this time I can succeed, maybe I can make a better start —ah, it may well be that the bowels have emptied, but this is deceptive. For the Esraris it is somewhat different. For an Esrari who has perfectly voided his bowels, time stops. This is a moment that says I have voided, I have moved apart from humans. Arrested time is one of the doors that open to the absolute. I wonder how many Esraris have been able to reach this door.

September 18, 2000

Where does the name of the Esraris come from?

From time to time everybody looks at the surrounding universe and is puzzled. Amazed, they say "Good God!", but soon forget the question and go on about their business. The Esraris are those who get stuck in the mystery of this moment. Everybody else forgets this moment; the Esraris do not. Did you say "solving the mystery of existence"? By no means; the Esrari knows that he cannot solve it. But he does not want to forget what he has seen. To be a silent part of this mystery that everybody witnesses, this is what makes the Esrari an Esrari, this insistence on the mysterious.

September 18, 2000

All in vain?

Can we describe Esrarihood to those who have just joined us? The Esraris are those who can imagine how the earth was before humans. They are those who ask what changed after humans arrived. For those who can imagine the state of the earth before humans, the answer is "nothing." If you look at history—the inkwell of our drivel—you cannot find any other answer. Before he died, the famous philosopher Schopenhauer left a note saying, "Well, that was close." Was it in vain for us to make this pact where we agreed to ceaseless progress? Yes. Is there something that can be done about it? No. So is this futility all for naught? Those who say "Yes, it is," are definitely not Esraris. For the Esraris, this futility is not all in vain. The Esraris, who have been able to see humanity's progressivist pact from the outside, have seen the beauty of absolute unity. For them, there is nothing else to say to those who harbor the illusion that "we are progressing" except "give me a break," and "towards what exactly are we progressing?"

September 18, 2000

The traveling Esrari looks around.

The Western traveler cannot unite with nature. He assumes that they have parted ways forever, and can never be reunited. "Ah," he says as he looks at nature, "I was one with you once upon a time." Whereas when the Esraris travel, there is a reunion, for they are made from the same substance after all. "I," says the Esrari to nature, "am together with you." It is easy to understand the loneliness of the Western traveler, if only somebody could understand the loneliness of the traveling Esrari!

September 1, 2000

The beautiful aspects of existence.

It is not as if existence does not have its defects; it does. There are times when God forces you to ask, "Why did you create me?" The answer lies behind some doors. Those doors are opened by the beautiful aspects of existence. Let us assume one day nihilism's tiresome task of enlightenment will be successful: on that happy day when everybody finally understands that all is futile, the one thing that will remain unchanged is absolute beauty. It is strange, but the nihilism of the Esraris ends when the absolute reveals itself. The Esraris are a community that does not like to keep the doors closed.

September 1, 2000

For the Esrâris, a clean mouth is paramount.

A clean idea cannot reside in an unclean mouth. The cleaning and rinsing of saliva is a moment of fresh beginning. There! You are innocent enough to begin anew, your mouth is fresh. You pause for a bit, anticipating the end of this brief moment brought on by the saliva seeping in and making the mouth dirty again. The ineffable idea begins forming in the rinsed mouth, but then quickly dissipates. For the Esraris, the cleansing of the mouth is performed several times a day in order to attain a brief pause cut short by the saliva's onrush. Moreover it is educational, squeezed in between the moment just before the filth of existence and the moment just after. Right now I am clean, but soon I will be filthy because I am human. As I become filthy they say "he is living," and in that brief moment of cleanliness they say "he has paused, he is looking."

September 1, 2000

Shortbreads.

It has been fifteen years. In Eski Foça, just next to what is now the Teachers' Association building, there was a bakery that sold shortbreads. One day fifteen years ago, the bathers who emerged from the sea to buy shortbread saw two trays of it in the shop window, one tray in the front and another behind it, but the shop was closed. The shortbreads were laid out in the usual manner.

Today, fifteen years later, these shortbreads are still sitting there. It turns out the baker had died, and his children, thinking that the shortbread had killed their father, decided to leave it out as a deterrent. For fifteen years the cookies have been sitting in detention. The baker is gone but his shortbread remains fossilizing in its trays, reminding the neighbors about the fate of their maker. They had been created for one reason, but their duty has changed. They have succeeded in freezing time since their owner has died. These are the only cookies in the world that have such an existential duty.

August 24, 2000

Yakamoz.*

For that evanescent metaphysical stillness:

It rains and you get wet

Vay aman

The sun rises and you vanish

Vay aman

You insist on moonlight

Vay aman

You are the yakamoz.†

August 24, 2000

---

* "Yakamoz" is sea sparkle.

† Yusuf Hayaloğlu

0% commission fee charged for credit cards.

"Zero percent commission fee" is used to describe an absence, but because the zero commission fee is "charged," the zero has a presence here, this zero is such a creature that if it lifts its head up a little, it grows, and if it lowers its head a bit, it shrinks. Zero owes its being to this balance that should not be upset, it should position itself so that it will neither increase nor decrease, and know no possibility other than itself. This is the destiny of zero. Food for thought: maybe this is why it is round, as if it bows to everyone who comes and goes. Those who come, do they know where they arrive? No. Those who go, do they know where they are going? They do not know either. Then zero will stay where it belongs, as if in a state of peace and justice brought on by having lived for a very long time. An older man who is a close friend of the Esraris, upon hearing an Esrari say "Destiny," responded "I prefer to call it 'what is written on my forehead'* since I can touch my forehead." The moment of destiny: it neither increases nor decreases, but it simply exists, anyone can touch it. Zero, the mysterious number of the Esraris.

August 24, 2000

---

* "What is written on the forehead" is synonymous with destiny.

Beneath the sea, the moment when all hope is lost.*

It has struck the bottom of the sea. Nothing can be done except sit and wait to be rescued. In the vast surrounding water visibility is one to two centimeters. There is nothing else to do but sit and wait. Life has now lost its entertaining façade, the struggle has ended, the day has slunk away, lovers will never reunite. That single moment! The moment when the unity disintegrates in the face of the void. Those who could not foresee this void beyond the entertaining diversions of life cannot bravely greet this moment that ends all hope beneath the sea. Those who cannot withdraw into their own futility can only understand the true value of unity when this moment arrives and all hope is lost. They are not Esraris. The Esraris carry the void in their pocket. Yes, life is futile, but unity is beautiful. The Esraris are tranquil, because that void is divine.

August 17, 2000

* All hope is lost for the 116 sailors who were in the Russian nuclear submarine Kursk that sunk in the Barents Sea near the North Pole on 12 August 2000.

Is it easy to be İbrahim Tatlıses?*

He was born in a cave and the only blessing he acquired without an ordeal is his voice. He knew the value of this voice and he has become famous for it. His is not the story of someone challenging their fate, but the story of someone living it. Because of this, his astonishment is greater than ours. At first, he does not understand how this divine wheel spins. This is why he sings better than everybody else, because his need to understand is greater. When he turns around and looks behind, it is impossible for him not to see that cave. He has leapt out of some divine crevice and landed in the midst of all this. Since the eyes mirror the heart, it appears that he looks at this place from the beyond. But is it easy? He is an Esrari, torn from his branch, dragged by the wind. He needs unity more than others. No one but he himself holds his hand. No, it is not easy.

August 9, 2000

* İbrahim Tatlıses is a popular folk/arabesque music singer.

Once there lived another Esrari, also a poet.

Ali's Secret[*]

Should you desire to attain Ali's Secret
Seek the Wise Initiator ye Brethren
Should you desire to enter the Heart's Kaaba
Plunge into the Depth ye Brethren

He Existed when the Asserters Assembled[†]
He Is Our Beloved in the Rightful Truth
He Is the Secret Hidden in the Whole Universe
Attain the Secret of this Discipline ye Brethren

A Lesser Servant of this Way is the Esrari
Bearing Pearls of Learning and Lore
The Way of Ali is the Way of Humanity
Enter from Heart to Heart ye Brethren

August 5, 2000

---

* The poet Esrari.

† The event that is called *bezm-i elest* (the assembly of the asserters) refers to the gathering of spirits during which God has asked "Am I not your Lord?" to which the spirits have replied "Yes, you are."

The European Union according to the Esraris.

They do not use these exact words, but what they are essentially saying is: "As free individuals we will express ourselves freely." The question that the Esraris ask is this: "so when that happy day comes around, what will all of you express? What kind of individuals will you be?" This is a muddle. To this day, has there ever been a revolution that convinced you that its success would produce an authentic individual? What everybody demands in unison is a calendar that shows the future, an SUV to drive and the latest trend to wear. The Esrari sees the hand that reaches towards us and pressures us to "change" and individualize away from our familiar collectivity. The concept of *dayı* will go out the window, everyone will become an *amca*.* When we change we will be like them, we will perish by getting richer. Those who say "So be it" are not Esraris. The Esraris do not say "I will become an individual"; instead, they say, "I am raw, I have a long way to mature." The true friends of the Esraris will always come from the victims of fate, from those who have no other choice but to submit to fate. Turkey's only hope is its poor people.

August 3, 2000

* In Turkish, your paternal uncle is *amca* and your maternal uncle is *dayı*, while in English there only exists the word uncle. Without these nuances, familial relationships would lose context.

Is it possible to have such a thing as a manic Esrari?

Theoretically it should not be possible, but since fate bears us gently, and the Esrari submits himself to its current, then the impulse of "I need to give this thing in front of me a good shove" should not be present among the Esraris. But the phenomenon is chemical, gives no heed to theory, it just comes. Something ignites it, it breaks loose, the rage surges up, and the Esrari wants to give all of it a good shove. In moments like this, the Esrari must know how to withdraw. If there is no flint, the rage cannot spark and ignite. Withdrawal is the tradition of Esrarihood. The Esrari withdraws, watches and weighs, at least sometimes. The outburst is subdued in the gentle current. The mania ends, the gusts abate, the Esrari recovers.

August 2, 2000

The Esraris know this futility the best.

Look, son! An Esrari elder once said this to his child: "Life is a struggle, whatever you can grab profits you." Do not wait for that day to come, that day is Godot, it does not come. After all, you will end up dying "on the day before." Politics is drivel, it flows continuously, it is a bunch of cheap words. The Esraris, on the other hand, are those who show the courage of not drooling thus. But when everybody is making their way towards that appointed day, how will the Esraris endure, since they have torn the calendar pages from their notebooks? Is this what you are asking? Listen! There are two ways: elitist terrorism and marginal Sufism. The Esraris choose marginal Sufism. They record, for the act of recording is fundamental for them. You keep your heart clean—the game was never fun, but the key is to see the truth, son!

July 31, 2000

Who are these Esraris anyway?

For the Esraris, morning is when life awakens, and the setting of the sun is an ending. To live this ending as if it were a beginning is not something that the Esraris can handle, so they go to sleep. A good sleep, a good morning. This is the Esrari way to mature the spirit. Esraris like looking, and looking is at its most lovely in the morning. No sense of bedazzlement is as strong as that which is felt in the morning light. The Esrari's bedazzlement, which is felt in the morning light, is a powerful one.

July 28, 2000

Listen, son!

Listen, son! Language is sacred. The crackling of fire was considered the first poem of the Indic peoples. The Esraris consider man's first grunt in the face of the void to be the first poem, but it is the same thing really, there is no difference. That is, there was a grunting first and someone took heed of the crackling fire, listened to it, understood, and recorded that crackle as the first poem in his mythology. If language is sacred, the ear is the first principle. The faithful believe in this, that God's ear is everywhere. Even if nobody else hears the tree falling in the forest, He hears.

It is because language is sacred that if it dominates the ear, it loses something of its sanctity. It chases its ambition, becomes vulgar, ceases to be language, becomes tyrannical. Why could the Esraris never produce a dictator? If you understand this, you will have taken the first step towards Esrarihood.

This is my advice to the young.

July 24, 2000

The ear.

There is a saying among the Esraris that goes like this: "He who does not have ears does not have friends." You might say something, and if he does not hear you, you might as well have not said anything at all. If you are speaking to someone who does not have ears, you are on your own. Those who do not have ears are alone as well. Maybe it is only a pair of ears that two people expect from each other, and a perfect concord between these ears and the brain. It is this concord that the Esraris believe in, for without it the void prevails, the unity is broken. The rule of thumb is simple: guarantee the ear and the rest will follow.

July 21, 2000

The olive according to an Esrari elder.

The Esraris admire the olive tree. It is a tree that stands just as it is, it is resilient, and cannot bore into rock like the fig, but it holds on, anchoring itself over many years. It bears all the secrets and benevolence of its location, it bears the fruit of goodness. If you search, it is possible to find a malevolent sycamore, but you cannot find an ill-disposed olive tree. If it claims that it wants anything for itself, it is lying to protect somebody.

July 20, 2000

That raging drool of man.

Is it possible for an Esrari who defends goodness not to see his own drooling? But slobbering into a pot is not a tradition of the Esraris. An Esrari cannot accept human drooling. Saliva calls one to victory, "march," it says, "advance, advance and you will see." Those who advance are not Esraris. Esraris do not advance, for they know that there is nothing ahead to see. What they would see there is no different from what they see here. "Stop," one Esrari elder has said, "and you will see your fate from where you stand."

July 18, 2000

The advice of an Esrari elder.

When you win, do not make the defeated kneel before you. If the defeated kneels down on their own, it is customary to lift them up by their hand. If the victor has pride, so does the defeated. The just thing is for the defeated and the victor to stand as two people: as the defeated and the victor; as the victor and the defeated. This is the real triumph—the whole purpose of the exercise. Humankind has been molded from a single substance, and the same substance cannot be both victorious and defeated.

July 11, 2000

Submitting to the heat is necessary.

When the heat takes over a person, this person will cut the branch he is sitting on. Of what use is it to sit on this branch in this heat? Just cut it off! In order to safely climb down from the branch and to see that which seems to be progressing is in fact static, we need to submit to the heat. One can resist the cold, but one cannot resist the heat. The cold will leave one all alone against the emptiness, whereas one who submits to the heat submits to the unity. When one resists the void one is singular, one has potency. However, when one submits to the unity, one is really one in a million, powerless.

The heat in Ingmar Bergman's *The Silence* throws the heroes into a country where they do not speak the language. The disintegration they experience is the disintegration of the West, which is used to withstanding the cold: "Oh dear, it turns out that even language did not exist!" The Westerner dreads this, whereas for the Easterner the heat reveals the unity of existence against the emptiness. In order to witness this, it is enough to submit to the heat.

July 8, 2000

The shortcomings of existence.

There are people who have devoted themselves to seeing the shortcomings of existence. Nobody can console them, because they consider even consolation as a defect. This is a style used only by those who have completely lost their sense of faith. It is only they who think that they have split off from existence, never to be reconciled again. This gives rise to a panic, and the panic feeds a narcissism that soon figures out that everything is defective. On the other hand, for someone who pursues the possibility of surrendering to existence, who believes in the unity of existence so much as to never be able to find a defect in it, it is not the shortcomings but the beauties of existence that matter. There is one thing that cannot be buried under defects, and that is the beauty of the absolute.

July 6, 2000

Addressing the emptiness.

On the Internet "neither does the poet shed a tear, nor does the minstrel weep."* It can be argued that the Internet is only new, that it will change in the future, but as seen from the tasks that those who rule the world ascribe to the Internet, this situation is not likely to change. If it goes on like this, in the future those people who do not use the Internet will be more wholesome than those who use it. Why would those who have something to say choose to proceed on this complex "highway" that has millions of turns? Humankind, in the face of the void, is only in a state of unity. An Internet in the style of the one, which is being pushed by those who rule the world breaks the unity, destroys the whole mysticism of the void. If you are addressing the void, this means you have understood nothing about the void.

July 6, 2000

* From "The Shepherd's Fountain" by Faruk Nafiz Çamlıbel.

Eyes are mirrors of the heart.

On the Internet we chat without seeing each other's eyes, by using language. How many of us can use their language as mirrors of their hearts? Very few. Very few of these famous long distance friendships address the heart. There is also another issue: how many of us can believe what the other is saying without seeing their eyes? Again, very few. Looking for happiness in the paradise of average intelligence, this is what we do on the Internet. A massive arithmetic system that calculates the mean of humanity, this is the Internet. You have to use it well to understand that it takes the average. Before, those who could use their tongue as the mirror of their heart would write books. That is valuable; the Internet can never surpass the book. All this excitement is pointless.

July 6, 2000

Ahmet Güntan was born in İzmir in 1955. *First Blood.*, his first book of poems, was published in 1984, followed by *Sparkling Blood in Fog.* (1989), *Voyager 2* (together with Lale Müldür, 1990), *Romeo and Romeo.* (1995), *Paired Repetition.* (1999), *Court Book.* (2005), and *Collected Poems.* (2008). In 2011, he published *Fragmental Crude.*, a manifesto in which he voiced the need for a new kind of poetry. He is the author of three collections of essays, two novels, and co-founder of *Cehd* (2006), a poetry fanzine, and *Mahfil* (2008), a weekly magazine of poetry. He has been working as a smallpress publisher of poetry and prose since 2011.